Long Dark Night

*A long journey through
a dark night of the soul*

M. S. Aldrich

ISBN: 978-1-7385156-2-2

Author's Note

Writing poems has really helped me through the healing process. They are real and raw; I'm sharing my story in the hope it helps you through yours.

ALSO BY THE AUTHOR

Darkness Has Fallen

*Darkness has no power over those
who hold light.*

To my dad, for all your love and support, thank you. We have been through many ups and downs in life but we always manage to laugh and smile together.

Love you lots.

DARK NIGHT OF THE SOUL

Going through a
Dark night of the soul
I feel so empty lost
And alone
The world looks dark
And I feel so cold
My youth has gone
And I feel old

Going through a
Dark night of the soul
Everything went wrong
And I cannot move along
Or even know where I belong
Anxiety fear
And depression
Fills me here

Going through a
Dark night of the soul
Where did the sun go
Where is the light
Nothing but darkness
To surround me now
No one sees this
Or feels my pain

It's all internal
And I'm full of shame
Why can't I heal
Why can't I smile
I've been going through this
For such a long time
Every time I think
This is coming to an end
Another dark shadow
Engulfs me again
Round and round
Backwards and forwards
Again, and again
Another layer to deal with
Yet another pain
I hope and pray
Only one more lessen
To learn
Then I can heal
And be me again
I don't know
Where I'm heading
And I don't know
What to do
One thing I'm sure of though
I'll never give up hope

IT STARTED WITH GRIEF

It started with grief
The pain was too much to bear
So, I hid it away
Inside myself
So no one could see it
I hid it so well
I forgot it was there
Carried on going
Struggling along
With illness
And pain
Buried in there
It turned into anger
But I didn't know why
Then it turned into fear
Way too much to bear
I lived in turmoil
And despair
Couldn't cope with life
So, I hid away
Isolated and lonely
And suffering every day
Plus, the troubles of life
And other people's pain
Sent me into chaos
Too much did I care

But I had to hide away
From them
To give me some time
cause
Mine was already too much
But to feel theirs as well
I kept on distracting myself
From the pain
Tried so hard to numb
Numb the feelings away
Until it was time
To face it all
Couldn't go on suffering
That isn't fair
So, I go within
To heal all the hurt
Fill myself with love
That I really deserve
my love to heal
 and repair
my broken heart
my precious gem
no more hiding
or running away
because I deserve peace now
and no more pain

LIFE IS A STRUGGLE

Life is a struggle
And I'm not doing well
Sometimes I can't cope
And it feels like hell
My body doesn't function
As best as it can
And my mind
Is in chaos
Doesn't make sense
My heart is still broken
So much pain
So much grief
That I can't explain
Don't even remember
When it began
Now I've come a long way
But still a long way to go
Seems this healing journey
Will never end
And the hurt never goes
Struggling along
From day to day
Some days are harder
And others
Don't feel so wrong
I know no one can save me

Or fix all that's wrong
It's my responsibility
To create a better life for me
And learn how to heal
Sometimes it's hard though
But I can't stand still
I'm not staying here
Here in hell

FEELS LIKE I'M LOSING EVERYTHING

Feels like I'm losing
Everything that matters to me
Why?
Because of my phobias
And my C-PTSD
The things that happened
In the past
Are destroying me now
How do I overcome this
Just don't know
I've tried and tried
So very hard
To heal myself again
But the harder I try
The more I fail
Honestly getting nowhere
All this trauma from the past
I cannot overcome
It's in my mind
And my memories
It's in my body too
I tried so hard
To leave the past behind
But I'm losing everything now

Everything that matters to me
Even though
This isn't my fault
And life didn't go my way
It's up to me
To put things right
So, I don't lose everything
That matters to me

This Crisis Of Mine

I'm in a crisis yet again
Seems the story of my life
Why can't I be normal
And just get on with my life
Seems like everything's
A disaster
Even the littlest of things
So much chaos
And drama
It's all inside
This crisis of mine
Want to just close
My eyes
And never wake up
See I'm so tired
And feel like giving up
But here I am still surviving
Everything that happens to me
Why can't anything be simple
Or easy in life
Oh, what a dream
That would be

NUMB

When the pain
Is too hard to bear
And it hurts so much
You can't take anymore
You go numb
To preserve
Go numb to survive
When things are difficult
And you're overwhelmed
So much going on
And it's just too much
You go numb
So, you can't feel anymore
To keep you sane
From all the chaos
And mess
When you are afraid
And its too hard to cope
As the terror
Goes through you
You just make yourself numb
Just numb out it all
It's just too heavy
To carry that on
Going numb
So, you can't feel anything

It's like pausing

For a little while

It doesn't solve the problems

Long term

But it will help

You through

a little

when you are at your worst

Bad Hormones

These bad hormones
Are like little demons
They're seeping through my veins
They mess up my thoughts
And make me feel insane
All the tears start pouring
When they get inside my heart
The pain is so unbearable
I'd do anything to
Make them stop
My stomach keeps on churning
With all the bad feelings inside
Wish I couldn't feel anything now
Run away from this black void
When it's almost over
I feel relieved inside
But so very exhausted
As I've just battled to save my life
Now that month is over
I'll get on with my life
But I know those little demons
Will come back
To wreck my life

PURGING

Oh, this purging
What a state
My skin breaks out
Red blotches on my face
It's saying my body's not coping
With this surge
Of hormones
Rushing through my veins
Sick as a dog
And I just can't cope
Feel like I'm dying
Lost all hope
Upset stomach
My body is shaking
What do I do
Waves of fire
Roar through my body
From my toes
Up to my head
Please make it stop
Terror sears through me
Now I'm in hell
The tears are burning
I know this so well
Like red hot lava
I'm sweating so hot

Then to start shivering cold
I'm getting too old
To keep going through this
It makes me unwell
And I can't take anymore
Feels like I've been poisoned
But it's from myself
All these hormones
What a mess
One emotional storm
After another
I have no control
Wish it would stop
But I lay here and wait
Until it passes by
Completely exhausted
Now I need to rest
I feel battered and bruised
All over my body
And in my chest
I pray one day this all ends
And there's no more need
For me to purge

How Can I Be Happy

How can I be happy
With all this pain I'm in
Can't handle my emotions
Oh, this is wearing thin
I'm tired of always coping
And I'm sick of struggling
All I do is survive
Yet all I want is to live
Seems life is all about feelings
And everything points to within
I have tried and tried
My very best
To heal all this pain
It's hard and it hurts
To face these wounds
And really, I don't know
Where to begin
I've tried so many different ways
But nothing seems to work
I've read and read
So many books
All I do is learn
I write and write
All these poems out
Trying to let go of the past
But it's a never-ending battle

I'm running out of energy
And I'm running out of time
So, how can I feel happy
With all this pain I'm in

Stuck In A Hole

When I feel sad
But I cannot cry
I write a poem
I feel the emotion
In my stomach
It's full to the brim
And I'm not joking
There's so much pain
From the past
I can't let go
Or move on with my life
I'm stuck in a hole
That's dark and grey
So unhappy
Every single day
Why can't I move forward
And leave the past behind
Get with life
And be happy again
Life is short
And mine's wasting away
Just can't shift
All these greys
How do I get unstuck
Or move away
I'm tired and feel older

Than my years
It's been so long
Since I felt okay
I just want to feel happy
Feel the sun's rays
With a big smile
On my face
I need to get unstuck
And move on again

Filled with Fear

I can't live any sort of life
When fear is at the core
It eats away from the inside
And breaks me that's for sure
It doesn't actually make any sense
Why I feel this at all
I used to be so fearless
Nothing could shake
My soul
I lived a life
So happy
And adventures
Were my source
No one ever scared me
I could fight my battles well
But I now can't figure out
How I got so broke
I'm riddled with fear
Like being stuck in a horror film
But this is not what I chose
How do I change the channel
Or take my finger off pause
I feel so stuck
Stuck in a rut
Fear is my curse

RIDICULOUS

This just seems
So ridiculous
All these weird phobias
They really don't make sense
I suppose that's why
They're called irrational phobias
Feel crazy in my head
I have tried so many times
To heal them
But nothing ever works
This makes me feel so stupid
And totally ridiculous
When I speak out loud
And explain my phobias
It sounds so silly
In my logical mind
Yet the fear is real
As it runs through my veins
And all the chaos
It causes in myself
So many years wasted
It's just all so stupid
Silly and ridiculous
These phobias
Just make no sense
It's all so absurd

TRAPPED

I feel trapped
In this situation
And there's no way out
I'm kicking and screaming
Inside
But there is no sound
I'm crying on the inside
Yet no tears in sight
The fear is so overwhelming
Oh, I just want to shout
Feels like I'm going crazy
Makes no sense at all
Don't know how to handle
My emotions
Living in so much doubt
Nothing makes this better
Nothing soothes my soul
All I do is write
Write it all out
Only way I know how
To let go
And let stuff out
Otherwise
It stays trapped
Trapped inside myself

Depressed

I am so depressed
By all the emotions
I have suppressed
Feel so worn down
Under this dark cloud of mine
Everything seems pointless
And has no meaning
Just can't find any joy
Only when I'm dreaming
I find it hard to smile
And to laugh would be a blessing
But all I do is cry
Or inside I'm screaming
Can't pick myself up
Or see any sun shining
Everything's so grey
In a miserable life
With everything I do
I'm constantly frowning
And everything feels so hard
All motivation gone
And I don't feel inspired
When everything feels wrong
Only thing to do
Is learn to let go

MISUNDERSTOOD

I don't feel understood
And I feel like we can't relate
What I'm feeling
Or what I'm thinking
Seems no one's
On the same wavelength
And I'm feeling alone
I feel so isolated
When I feel misunderstood
Finding it hard to communicate
I feel everyone takes me wrong
It's like they don't really know me
If they did
They'd know my intentions
Are always good
Yet know one seems to get that
I always come from a place of love
They assume I'm always angry
But that isn't true
I'm always passionate
Mixed with frustration as well
Even when I try to help others
I always regret
Because they take me so wrong
I'm just so misunderstood
If only they knew

Just how much I cared
Then they would realise
I'm offering
Comfort, love and wisdom
I'm only trying to share

Paralysed By Fear

Paralysed by fear
I cannot move along
Paralysed by fear
Why can't I be strong
Paralysed by fear
Everything feels wrong
Paralysed by fear
Nowhere do I belong
Paralysed by fear
My heart bleeds on and on
Paralysed by fear
I cannot enjoy a song
Paralysed by fear
With others I cannot bond
Paralysed by fear
I cannot find joy
Paralysed by fear
I cannot feel loved
Paralysed by fear
All the light has gone
Paralysed by fear
Years have been wasted and gone
Paralysed by fear
Life just drags on
And on

SUFFERING WITH PHOBIAS

Suffering with phobias
Is no joke
The amount of fear
And terror
They evoke
Is unreal
It doesn't just affect the mind
And emotions
But the body too
Your whole being
Is in despair
And it makes you feel unwell
After the panic
And the fear has gone
You're left completely exhausted
From all of that chaos
Every time you are triggered
Or a panic comes on
The feeling of dread
And the doom
Is horrendous
Because you know
What's to come
So you spend your life avoiding
Everything
And anything that can trigger

The phobia itself
No matter how many times
You tell yourself
You are safe
Your body doesn't believe it
And won't cooperate
You have no control
So, there's only one thing to do
Is just let go
Let go of trying to control
You are wasting your time
You can't control or force
Your body to respond
How you want
It's being pumped with adrenaline
And cortisol
It needs time to repair
To calm down
On its own
To get back to normal
Nervous system regulated
Until the next time
You are triggered again
Trying to manage it
Is just futile
What you need
Is healing
To really overcome

Once and for all
Because living in dread
Is not great
And living in fear
Is no life at all
The only way to go
Is heal it at the root
What caused the phobia
Where did it start
Then change how you see it
Your perspective needs to change
Love yourself to heal the pain
So everything will heal
And you can live again

EXTREME EMOTIONS

Why do my emotions
Feel so extreme
They swallow me whole
Think I could drown
Oh, I want to scream
I'm either in a deep dark sadness
Or terror running through my veins
With so much frustration
All feels so real
Can't switch them off
And just go to sleep
Because even when I do
They creep into my dreams
Causing all kinds of nightmares
No escaping these
Seems nothing I ever do
Helps me to heal
How do I let go
And move along
Been trapped with these emotions
For a long time
And they're so extreme
I'm tired and weary
From these roller coaster rides
There is nowhere to run
And no way to hide
They're way too extreme

SO MUCH TRAUMA

I'm tired of battling
I'm tired of this fight
I live in terror
For most of my time
I have so much trauma
From the past
How do I let go
How can I heal this
It causes so much pain now
And destroys my life
Feels like nothing
Ever feels right
It's cold and dark
Inside myself
As if the lights have
Been switched off
And I'm left with this
No one can hear her
When she screams inside
No one can see
All the tears she hides
Feeling so alone
In this long dark night
And life is passing by
I feel so old
When is it time

That I can start
To live in hope
Because right now
I can't find the way
There's nothing but
Fear and tears
Getting in the way
And feels like
A never-ending task
Of clearing them away
Layer upon layer
Of trauma inside
Causing all this chaos
I just want to hide
All I really want is inner peace
Inner peace inside

Shattered Dreams

All my dreams
Have been shattered
Seems they're always
Out of reach
There are so many obstacles
Getting in the way
Which fills me with frustration
And turmoil
Each and every day
There's always something
That pops up
When things start moving forwards
Everything just gets messed up
When I set goals
I never reach the top
I only ever get so far
Then something
Pops in the way
And wrecks it all again
I try to climb over
Go under
Or move these obstacles away
But no matter how hard I try
I always end up stuck
And my dreams
Are out of reach

Just Floating Around

I'm just floating around
With no real place to go
I feel so lost
Just don't know what to do
I have no purpose now
And no direction
To take
And nowhere do I belong
Not even a clue
Why am I here
What's the meaning
Of life
The questions
I ask myself
No answers I can find
I'm sure there's a reason
Why I was put
On this earth
You can't just be born
To just float around
And nothing of worth to find
I will find that reason
And when I do
Happiness will
Shine out of me
As bright as the sun

And I'll still float around
But for a reason
And a purpose
I'll have direction

Irrational Fears

It's been such a long time
Since I felt
Comfortable, relaxed
And at ease
I can't even remember
 how that feels
On a good day
I still feel anxious or stressed
On a bad day
I feel so much fear
For things that
Make no sense
See irrational phobias
Or fears
Don't seem right
And somehow seem silly
In your rational mind
Yet emotionally and physically
Those fears are real
They make you want to
Run away and scream
This crazy madness
That makes no sense
And you feel out of control
Stuck in a bad dream
And you can't wake up

Or shake it off
It's so extreme
It is hell
Constantly searching for relief
Sometimes I lose hope
Of ever overcoming
These irrational fears
Of mine
It's like a faraway dream
Fears and phobias
How on earth do I heal

ALL I DO IS FAIL

I've tried so hard
To heal these things
But all I ever do
Is seem to fail
I've spent all this time
Trying to figure this out
But all I do is cry
I've tried so many different things
But nothing ever works
Why can't I find the answers
To the questions
I have in my mind
I cannot find a solution
To these problems
Of mine
Seems I'm going round in circles
Over and over again
I'm stumbling around
In the dark
And I cannot find my way
All I ever want
Is to heal my heart
Of this fear and pain
But no matter
How hard I try
All I do is fail

Grief Turned To Fear

Why did my grief
Turn into fear
I just don't know
Why this is so
How can all of this love
Turn into so much fear
Because that's what it is
You know
Grief is love
It's all my love
Yet my heart feels full of fear now
But also, empty as well
How can that be
I'm confused
About it all
Nothing makes sense
In this weird world
And I cannot get to grips
With this strange life
All these emotions
That I cannot control
Being human is odd
All these feelings
In an unstable void
So, I isolate
All on my own

My heart is full of fear
And I don't want anyone to know
Why can't I just feel safe again
In this weird strange life
That doesn't make sense
What a peculiar thing

UNHEALABLE

Unhealable
 is that even a word
I've no idea but that is
How I feel
I feel as if I'm unhealable
Unable to heal
I've tried so many things
And I've tried so hard
But whatever I do
I'm clearly not doing it right
Because I'm still in
 the same position
I've been in for a long time
I'm tired and weary
And I feel old
Like time is running out
And I'm feeling so cold
Why can't I heal
What am I doing wrong
Where did my love go
And how do I move along
The therapies I have tried
Over the years
Always seem to fail me
What do I do next
I'm going round in circles
But getting nowhere

FRANTIC

Sometimes my energy feels
So frantic
Too many different types
All at once
I feel like
I'm all over the place
And I can't relax
It feels like I need something
But I don't know what
It's like I'm franticly searching
For something else
I go upstairs
Then I want to come back down
I go outside
Then I want to come back in
I try to read
To distract my mind
But I can't concentrate
Or focus my mind
I don't know what I want
And I don't know what I need
All I can do is write it all out
This frantic feeling
Is a horrible state
Do I need to cry
Or shout it out

So many emotions
Flying around
All at once
I feel so confused
And I cannot cope
So frantic
Wish it would stop

Too Tired To Carry On

I just feel too tired
To carry on
I have no energy left
To keep fighting on
I feel so drained
No life left
In me now
I worked so hard
To keep going
And to try and heal my pain
But no matter how hard
I try
And no matter how long
I just keep failing
And I can't move along
I'm stuck in time
And I'm trapped in pain
All I ever do is cry
And I feel ashamed
Why can't I heal
And why can't I get better
Run out of motivation
All out of steam again
No amount of sleep or rest
Cures this exhaustion

WILL I EVER AGAIN

Will I ever stop crying
And be happy again
All I do is cry
These tears never seem to end
Will I ever feel safe again
All I do is panic
And I'm full of fear
Will I ever find peace
Ever again
I cannot relax
So much chaos in my head
Will I ever feel love
In my heart ever again
It feels so heavy
With all this pain
Will I ever see the light
Ever again
Everything looks dark
Think I'm in hell
Will I ever recover
Ever again
Been so poorly
For such a long time
Will I ever feel good again
Because I feel so bad
Inside myself
Over and over again

Invisible

I feel so invisible
In this world
Don't think anyone sees me
And I don't feel heard
If I just melted away
Would anyone notice I'm gone
Do I even exist
On this earthly plain
It all feels wrong
I feel so invisible
In this world
No one notices
Or sees my pain
Only I know
And that really hurts
No one can feel this
What's in my heart
So much sorrow
And it's gone so dark
I feel so invisible
In this world
Haven't found anything
To light back up
My world
So I can shine
And be seen again

IF ONLY

If only I could feel happy
But I feel so sad
Want to feel love
But I only feel fear instead
I need to feel at peace
But chaos rules my head
Wish I was healthy
But I'm poorly in bed
If only life was simple
There's too much mess
I really need to heal
But there's too much pain
I just want to feel good
Yet all I feel is bad
Wish I could relax
But there is too much stress
I want to feel alive
Oh, I'm feeling half dead
If only I could look forward
Instead of living in dread
I'd like to be successful
But all I do is fail
Wish I was confident
And not so full of shame
If only I could live my life
Instead of surviving this hell

Love And Fear
At The Same Time

How can you love someone
With all of your heart
Yet feel fear being with them
At the same time
How can you miss someone
When they're not around
Yet the anxiety hits
With just the thought of them
Being around
How can you want to be with someone
All of the time
But when you are
You panic
It makes no sense at all
How can you crave someone's company
Yet you want to be left alone
At the same time
How can you be so full of love
And yet so full of fear
At the same time

CLAWING MY WAY OUT OF HELL

I'm having to claw
My way out of hell again
This task isn't easy
In fact, it's hard as hell
It hurts so bad
That I want to scream out loud
The fire is burning
From within me
Please God help
Make this stop
Exhausted beyond belief
And I really don't feel well
I cannot see in front of me
As this darkness descends
Like a black smog
Covering my light
All I can hear are my screams
From within myself
The only things I feel are
Grief pain and fear
Happiness is just a far-off dream
That I can't even see
Sometimes I do see a glimmer
Of light
But only a glimmer
That doesn't last

Sometimes I think
I'm coming out from this dark
And things seem to be better
To then suddenly fall
Right back into the dark
So, I start crawling out
All over again
To claw my way out
Out of this hell
Each time feels harder
Than the last
I suppose I'm getting older
As time passes by
And I'm growing more tired
With each and every time

I Should Be Afraid Of Nothing Now

I should be afraid
Of nothing now
So many times
I've walked through
the fires of hell
I should be afraid of nothing now
For over two decades
I've been unwell
I should be afraid of nothing now
So many times
Have I proved my strength
I should be afraid of nothing now
How many times
I've faced these fears
I cannot count
I should be afraid of nothing now
In my dreams I met my demons
Faced those demons in my hell
Yet here I still am fighting
For my life
Filled with so much fear
I'm actually afraid of myself

Protection Response

I know you are trying to protect me
But I don't even know
What from
See there isn't a threat
Or real danger
Yet you make me feel
Like there is some
I try to ask you why
To find out what is wrong
I've begged and pleaded
So many times
Please let me hear you
In there
Tell me what is wrong
I don't understand
Why this happens
I have no idea what's wrong
But for some reason
You make me want to run
Run away screaming in terror
Yet there isn't a reason why
That I can make sense of
Why does my nervous system
Constantly keep turning on
Sending me into chaos
This is how my body responds

As though I'm in trauma
Even when there is none
My mind and body are
trying to protect me
from the threats
that are long gone
Now I'm safe and secure
but my brain
still thinks
there's something wrong
so, it sends these signals
that I'm under threat
and danger is all around

WISH I KNEW

I wish I knew
How to heal
Wish I knew how to let go
If only I could heal
And get better now
Wish I knew
The answers
To all of my questions now
If only I could move forward
And leave the past behind
Wish I knew the solutions
To all of my problems now
I'm tired
And I'm weary
All out of fight
But giving up
When I've come this far
Isn't an option now
Low moods
I can't lift my mood up
It's gone down too low
I'm in a dark place
Which is scary as hell
I look for some light
Until I can find my way
But I can't see a way forward

And I'm not going back
So, I sit here and wait
Until this dark mood passes
Not much else to do
I know I have my love
And inner strength
To help me through
So, no matter how low I go
I will always pick up my mood

NOTHING MAKES IT BETTER

Nothing makes it better
When I go down the drain
When my hormones kick in
I have no control
My moods are horrendous
Feel like I'm falling
Down a dark well
Trying to climb back up
But I'm all out of hope
So, I sit here and ponder
How did this all start
Do I need to heal
Heal my heart
Or is it purely physical
Oh, where do I start
I try to eat healthy
And as clean as I can
But it hasn't made that much difference
To my hormones or my mind
Whatever I try
And no matter what I do
Nothing makes it better
I'm in a big stew

ANXIETY

Sometimes I feel anxious
But I don't know why
Sometimes it comes on
For no reason at all
Sometimes I get triggered
Which I can understand
Because there's a reason
So, it seems defined
But when it starts without reason
I feel confused inside
Why does this happen
So many times
I'm tired of going through this
It just isn't right
It's a horrible feeling
Want to run and hide
Wish I could heal this
And feel alright
It feels like I can't
Trust myself
Or control how I feel
I just want to be happy
And free again

Unbelievably Tired Now

I'm so unbelievably tired now
I feel like I've had enough
My batteries are low again
And I'm running out of strength
I'm not getting any younger
The years are passing by fast
Feels like most of my life
Has been wasted
On not feeling well
And I missed out on so much
This illness has taken over
And ruined my whole life
I'm just so unbelievably tired now
Not sure how much more
I can take

FAILED AGAIN

I'm so confused
And full of doubt
That I'll ever heal
Or get better again
Just want to scream and shout
My hope has gone now
Can't see a way out
Trapped inside myself
And stuck in this drought
I just can't heal
No matter how hard I try
Could just cry out
Why didn't it work
I did my best
Yet another therapy
That didn't help
Just another failure
Oh, what a mess
I cannot find
Got so many questions
The answers
I cannot find
It's causing so much stress
I'm going out of my mind
No one seems to know
What's going on within

Nothing makes sense
So, maybe it's just as well
I've been searching
For a long time
For little signs or clues
But I can't see any
Maybe I've gone blind
Always in chaos
My emotions and my mind
My life is like a storm
All the frustration causes tears
The answers I can't find
 to my questions
how do I heal
how do I get better
before I run out of time
My nervous system
is dysregulated
and I cannot feel calm
always turned up high
nerves so fragile
constantly on alert
for no reason at all
Always fretting
always out of control
I feel shaky and trembly
At the slightest of things
Always on alert

Waiting for something to go wrong
And the flash backs
Are never gone
Triggers are everywhere
Oh, this feels so wrong
Why can't I find these answers
On how I can heal

Horrible Hormones

Feeling really sick
And an upset stomach too
My body is aching
And fatigued again as well
My brain's not functioning properly
Feels like I'm insane
One emotional storm
After another
Oh, what do I do
Want to be alone
And curl up in a ball
Too tired to cope
Under the duvet I go
Hiding from the world
But I can't hide from my demons
They're under the duvet too
As the tears start to come
I'm writing all of this to you
Because really
I have no idea what else to do
Got a hot water bottle
On my stomach
To try and stop the pain
No, it's not just the physical
But the emotional as well
Sipping on some ginger tea

Trying to stop the nausea
Oh, I'm crying again
I've been eating so healthy
But now it was in vain
Because all I want
Is chocolate and chips
Oh, it's all so strange
Don't want to talk to anyone
Just leave me all alone
This shit I carry is heavy
And I need to let it go
Keep trying to find a cure
Keep trying to heal this pain
I'm going round in circles
This cycle never ends

My Way

I don't know what I want
And I don't know what I need
Complete and utter despair
Is all I ever feel
So full of emotions
Oh, this shit is real
I'm like a walking ticking time bomb
Any minute I could explode
 need to let go of this pain
I'm hurting so bad
And drowning in all this rain
I write all this out
Not even sure why
But it somehow feels natural
So, think this is just my way

I Sink Into A Dark Place

Sometimes
well, quite often
I sink into a dark place
For no seemingly good reason at all
It's like a big dark cloud
Swallows me whole
I can't get out
Or stop it
I have no control
It's a scary place
When it's inside yourself
Like a great big void
Or a big black hole
I slowly fall down
And there's nothing to hold
No way of coming back up
All the light gone
Panic starts rising
Heart pounding in my chest
As sweat pours out
And I'm burning in the heat
Think I'm in hell now
Oh, what a mess
All I can do
Is wait for it to pass
As it always does

What Do I Do Now

What do I do now
When everything's so hard
My life is in bits
And my hearts broken apart

What do I do now
When everything I try
To heal to get better
Never works
And it's a waste of time

What do I do now
When I can't seem
To find
Something to make me feel good
To make everything right

What do I do now
When all I can do is cry
Everything looks dark
And I've forgotten how to smile

It Is What It Is

It is what it is
Well what else can I say
No point beating myself up
For feeling this way
I'm tired and hurting
And I cannot move along
Too many disorders
To battle on and on
I've run out of steam
Exhausted and overwhelmed
Is all I seem to be
Just trying to overcome
Trauma, sickness, phobias
It's all too much for me
There's so much pressure
To be well
This stress makes me more poorly
Trying to carry on
Trying to fit in
Always wishing to be normal
And praying to be well
But after all this time
I doubt I ever will
So, all I can say for now is
It is what it is

PANIC ATTACKS

I don't know why I suffer from panic attacks
But I wish they'd go away
Why can't I stop them
Why can't I heal
This pain
It feels like fire inside
Feel like I've gone to hell
This fire engulfs me
Filling me whole
Or is it cleansing
Now there's another thought
Maybe this fire is cleansing
Cleansing my soul
Maybe this is healing
Who would have thought
If I just let it happen
Instead of running away
But the fear is just too much
And I cannot live that way

How Many More Times

How many more times
Will I feel this way
Had my heart broken
Yet again

How many more times
Will I suffer this way
So many dark shadows
Around and within me

How many more times
Will I feel unwell
So much illness
Can't take this again

How many more times
Will I have to pick myself up
I'm down on the ground again
And exhaustion won't let me up

How many more times
Will I have to cry
To let out this pain
Surely my well has dried up by now

How many more times
Will I try to heal
To only realise
I haven't healed a thing

RUN

Sometimes I just want to run
Run away from life
Never stop running
Run forever
Never look back

Sometimes I just want to run
Run away from all this strife
'Cause nothing's ever easy
Just run away and hide

Sometimes when I'm overwhelmed
And nothing's going right
All I want to do is run
Run for my life
Just run and run
And never stop for breath

So Completely Lost

I'm so completely lost
And I've no idea what to do
I spend my time
Wondering around
With no real place to go
When I focus on my healing
And getting myself right
But I'm going at snail pace
A tiny bit at a time
Bit by bit
Day by day
And night by night
When I stop doing the healing stuff
And take a look around
I realise my life
Lacks meaning
And purpose
I cannot find
So lost and empty
That truth hits me in the eyes
So, I turn myself back around
And concentrate on the healing
Practices again
Not looking out at my world
I don't know what else to do now
Feel like I'm wasting time

The years have passed so quickly
And my youth
Has now but gone
I don't know where I'm going
And I don't know what I want
I hope I make my mind up soon
Before my time runs out

HIDING THIS HELL

I've been hiding this hell
For so many years
Behind my crooked smile
There are so many tears
So much pain
Behind the laughter
Oh, what a disaster
With all of this fear

Hiding this hell
So no one can see
Pretending I'm okay
I'm even lying to me
Which makes me ashamed
You see

Putting on a brave face
Hiding behind the makeup
While drowning in emotions
Like a current under the sea
Always gasping for breath
So close to death
Faking being okay

Feel like I'm always in danger
But there is none

I can't shift those feelings
It's all so wrong
Trapped in a nightmare
Stuck in hiding this hell

ANOTHER THERAPY

I started another therapy
My mentor is nice
I was making good progress
Then my hormones came
And washed it away
Back to the beginning
Start all over again
Undoing my hard work
My mood is so low
Now I have to pick myself up
This therapy seems good
And makes so much sense
So, I'll carry on trying
Until I succeed

BLOCKED

I feel this blockage
Inside myself
It's there in my stomach
And it causes hell
I wish I could shift it
But not sure how
I don't even know what it is
But it's been there a long time
Creating havoc for myself
It makes me unwell
And it makes me feel bad
If only I could release it
And get on with my life
It's dark and black
That's all I can sense
I know it doesn't belong there
Inside myself
I just don't know how to move it
Or how to let it go
But I need to find a way
Can't stay blocked forever more

FRUSTRATION

Oh, this frustration
is eating me up alive
balling me up into knots
I'm seething inside
Why can't I figure this out
My phobias are ruining
And completely destroying
My life
I can't live this way anymore
Avoiding things
Isn't the way to go
I've tried so hard to heal
And overcome this fear
But nothing ever works
Over twenty odd years
Of therapy and learning
Yet here I still am
Still in the same despair
Because I cannot heal
Or repair
It's cost so many pounds
Not to mention the energy
And time
I'm not getting any younger
Wasting precious time
I'm no better than I started

And still no clearer with all I've learned
Oh, this frustration
Is eating me up alive
And I fear I'll never again live
Live a real life

WILL I EVER GET BETTER

Will I ever get better
Will I ever heal
From this pain
I really don't know
But I feel I've gone insane
I'm tired and weary
Of struggling along
It's been so hard
Since you've been gone
Feels like nothing ever goes right
And I can't move along
I'm stuck in this cycle
Everything repeats
Over and over again
Can't deal with the anxiety
Or cope when panic sets in
Oh, and the depression
It's all too much for me
This isn't right
And it's just not fair
Wish this would end
So, I can start living
again

So Scared All Of The Time

Why do I feel so scared
All of the time
I'm so scared of so many things
In life
So, alone and isolated
From everyone
Yet I can't go anywhere
On my own
Can't do anything
That brings me joy
Paralysed and stuck
In a cycle
Of always being afraid
Always on alert
My body and brain
As if there's danger
And threats
That don't even exist
It's all imaginary in my mind
Yet it feels so real
Oh, what a mess
I think it's memories
From the past
But I hardly remember
Most of them
Yet my body does

And my brains in distress
I can't figure out anymore
How to feel safe
I think I have trust issues
With others
And myself
If only I could learn to trust again
And have more faith

ALL TOO MUCH

It's all too much
This life of mine
I get so overwhelmed
A lot of the time
I've so many feelings
So many sights, smells
And sounds
It gets too much
All this stimulation
Oh, I could just cry
It feels too hard to cope
And handle sometimes
I have all these emotions
That are so extreme
They take over everything
Don't even know
Who I really am anymore
Just drowning all of the time
All of this overwhelm
Just feels like too much

RUNNING

All I ever do is
Run away and hide
Don't want to face this
These feelings I have inside
Look away or shut my eyes
Close my ears
To all the sounds
Ignore, distract
And run away
Is all I know how
To respond
But no matter how hard I try
These ghosts from my past
Still reside
Yes, these ghosts, ghouls
And demons
Take away my light
It's dark and ever so scary
And days feel more like nights
How do I stop myself from running
Running from my life
How do I face these demons
Or let go
Of my horrible past?
Right so there is nothing
Else to do now

But give in and surrender
To this now
Let myself feel this pain
And let go
Yes, that's right
Face these demons head on
And give them love
And light
Fill myself with so much love
And turn this all around
Because no one else
Can do this for me
This was my task to figure out
Now I've found that wisdom
That came up from
My own self
Now there's one thing
That I'm sure of
Is you can't keep running
From your own life

DON'T KNOW WHERE I'M GOING

I don't know where I'm going
But I certainly know where
I've been
Been dragged through
The fires of hell
So many times
It's unreal
And so many times
I wanted to just scream
Yet I grit my teeth
So tightly
And I'm on my knees
Crawled through
With my bare hands
Oh, that pain is real
No one knows
Or hears me
This silence I do keep
All alone in this state
Not a place
I want to be
Don't know how many
More times
I'll have to go through it
Before I rise back up
My hearts been cracked wide open

And terror sears
Through my veins
And nothing ever stops this
I just wait for it to pass
There is no control
And no way to steer out
It always comes unexpected
And leaves
Leaves me in a drought
Nothing left inside
But a big dark void
So, I don't know where
I'm going
And I don't know what is next
All that really matters
Is I don't want to
Go there again

No One Sees

No one ever sees
What I go through
And that's why
I feel so alone
No one knows
How much it hurts
And no one else
 really understands
No one knows
how hard things are
all my blood, sweat
and tears
just to get this far
No one sees
how complicated this is
they are only looking
at one thing
they're focused on
and that's not even half
I have more than one problem
A few disorders
No one sees
How hard I try
To heal
I do my best
It takes up all my energy

Time and strength
Just getting through
Day to day
Is an ordeal
In itself

UNACKNOWLEDGED

I have spent every single hour
Of every single day
For the past two decades
Trying to get better
And heal all this pain
I have used every ounce of energy
And every ounce of strength
To survive
Every single day
I'm not going to lie
It's been hell

I suffered so much
Yet most has gone unnoticed
Unacknowledged
That hurts a lot
Like it was all in vain
I tried my best to heal
All of my pain
And I'm doing my best
To let go of the rain

Sometimes I think it's a miracle
That I'm even still alive
How I didn't just keel over
And that would be the end of my life

But here I still am
Oh, my body does ache
And my heart still cries

Heartache and illness
Has taken its toll
It took super-human effort
To get where I am now
But I will never give up
After coming this far
Even if no one acknowledges
What I went through
I can be proud of myself
Because I know
What I survived

EVERY SINGLE DAY

I don't think
There has been a single day
In the past two decades
That I haven't had a panic attack
Not a single day
In all of those years
Have I felt at peace
Or at ease
In my life
Every single day
Has been a battle
Or a struggle
Just to get by
Why is it so impossible
To have a nice day
Even if I could manage
To feel okay
Even when I'm not panicking
Anxiety fills the gaps
And if it's not those
Depression gets through those cracks
Every single day
My emotions are in chaos
My nerves are frayed
And I am exhausted
By the lot

CRY FOR ETERNITY

I could cry for eternity
And never smile again
Because no amount of tears
Relieve me from this pain
No matter how many times
I cry
I fill back up again
There's never ending tears
Flooding through myself
If only I could heal
And dry up all this rain
So, the sun could come back out
And I'd feel happy again
But right now
That's only a dream
Oh, I could cry for eternity

I Sometimes Wonder

I sometimes wonder
How I'm still standing
After everything I've been through
It's a miracle

I sometimes wonder
How I carried on
Through all of the pain
And suffering
For so long

I sometimes wonder
How I keep fighting on
Even though I'm exhausted
I keep battling along

I sometimes wonder
How I'm still alive
How my heart's still beating
When it feels like
It's been cut up with knives

I sometimes wonder
How I'm still breathing
After these illnesses
My body caved in

And just couldn't function

Yet here I still am

I'M DONE

I'm done with this suffering
And I'm done with this pain
It's so unfair
I'm going insane
No one should have to suffer
Like this
We should be able to be happy
And healthy
As our birth right
My soul is crying
The tears stained my face
My body is hurting
And my heart's broken to bits
So very tired
Can't even think straight
It's just a constant battle
A never-ending fight
Between my heart and soul
And my mind
I can't bring myself into harmony
Or find inner peace
Inside is so noisy
And nothing makes sense
I'm so sick and tired
On and on, this repeats
Again

and again
Oh, I don't like my life
All I can say now
Is I am done

STRANDED

I feel like I'm stranded
Somewhere all alone
Or left on a desert island
With no hope
It's not a nice place
And I feel so cold
There are waves hitting hard
Struck by a storm
I'm tired of battling this fight
And I'm scared I'm losing
All my might
It's really dark
Dark as night
Been here for so long
And I'm running
Out of time
I feel so old now
My youth has gone
Wishing for a lifeboat
It's too far to swim
I tried my best
But it's looking pretty grim
What do I do now
When I feel stranded somewhere
All alone
On this desert island

I just want to go home
But wherever that is
I'm unsure
I need love and comfort
Somewhere to belong
But think it's too much
Too much to ask for

I Just Want To Go Home

I just want to go home
Where I belong
I'm tired of searching
And feeling alone

I just want to go home
Where it's warm
Sick of this world
I feel cold to the bone

I just want to go home
Where there is love
Can't find any here
I've just had enough

I want to go home
Where there is comfort
And care
Because so far here lately
I haven't found none

I want to go home
Where there's happiness
All I have now is
Fear pain and sadness

I just want to go home
Where there is peace
No more fighting
Or defending myself

I just want to go home
Where there is truth
I'm tired of being let down
And lied to
I need honesty and certainty

I just want to go home
Where there is light
Can't find my way here
It's as dark as night

ALL OUT OF WORDS

I'm all out of words now
Nothing left to say
As I stare out of the window
Just stare into space
Nothing but the sound
Of ringing in my ears
Nothing makes sense
Even after all these years
Feeling hopeless
 and all out of faith
Feeling all alone
even when I'm surrounded by others
in this world
this awful place
What else can be said
When there's nothing but pain
All out of words
Nothing left to say

FEAR

Fear destroys everything
It stops you from
Doing the things you want

Fear won't let you be
Who you want to be
It prevents you from
Being the real you

Fear traps you
From being free
It cages your spirit
And confines you

Fear makes all joy cease
To exist in you
It takes away your light
Leaving you in the dark

Fear puts you in a corner
Unable to move forward
Frozen to the spot
Time stands still
Yet the clock still ticks on

Fear cuts you off
From love
Leaving you feeling
Lost and alone
Complete disconnection of
Everything you love

Fear brings chaos
And destruction
No peace left in your soul
Just a silent noise

Fear leaves you empty
Yet full to the top
So full of fear
But empty of love

Fear keeps you stuck
You can't go where you want
Or do what makes you smile

Fear isn't good
Over ride it with love

I'll Never Give In
Or Ever Give Up

Whenever I think
Things are getting better
I always fall flat on my face

I pick myself up
Over again
Carry on going
Just doing my best

Then comes yet another hurdle
That I have to climb
It's hard and it hurts
But this I have to face

Every time I start
I start to see the light
A dark shadow
Comes along
And I cannot see my way

All the times
I've been let down
And nothing's going right
I've had to keep my faith

When all was lost
My heart broken to pieces
And nothing made any sense
Hope was all I had

So many times
When things were tough
I had to dig deep
For my inner strength

For all the times
When I've been down
And tears covered my face
I had to let them flow
So, I could let go
Of all the hurt and pain

I need to fill myself up
With all of my love
And never give in
Or ever give up
No matter what

NO MATTER WHAT DON'T QUIT

There's been so many times
I wanted to just quit
Wave a white flag
High in the air
When it all got too much
Too much to bear
I couldn't cope
With all the pain in there
It got so severe
For me on my own
I needed some help
From someone who knows
But whenever I asked
I got rejected from them
So many doors
 slammed in my face
I didn't feel worthy
Of help or advice
So much for
The caring profession
They didn't care at all
So, I'm trying my best
To heal all the hurt
Researching
And researching
And never giving up hope

I keep fighting
And fighting
To be heard
But it falls on deaf ears
So, I'll figure it out
All by myself

Now I'm getting a bit better
And I've learned so much
I'm proud of myself
Because I didn't quit
And I'm still here
To tell the tale
Of how I survived
And got stronger
And stronger
As time went by
I've grown so much
Coming out of the dark
And into the grey
Looking forward
For the light some day
I now have hope
And restored my faith
That another new life
That I can create
To be happy and healthy
Is all I asked

But now I know my worth
I'll do better than that
Then, I'm going to help others
Who are in a dark place
Show them how
To find their light again
So, they can heal
And find their own peace
So, they never quit
Finding their strength
To live a happy life
That they also deserve

DON'T STOP

If you are going through hell
Please don't stop
Carry on going
I know it hurts a lot
But please don't stop
I know it's hard
But don't give up
If you can't see the light
Just look up
Don't stay where you are
Please don't stop
Open your heart
Let the pain pour out
Cry, scream
Or even shout
But just don't give up
I know it's exhausting
Take a nap
And rest up
Take some time out
For yourself
Just don't stop
Keep moving forwards
Don't stop

THE DARK TIMES WILL END

I wrote all these poems
During my darkest of times
I didn't think I'd make it
Lost all my faith
And didn't realise I was strong
Just wanted to give up
Because it lasted so long
It was hard
And painful
Yet I carried on
Gritted my teeth
And bent my head down

I always knew
Somewhere inside
That this chapter would end
And I'd move on
That I'd heal my pain
Even though everything
Felt wrong
That I'd somehow make it through
That I am strong
Writing has helped me
And I'm sharing
With you
I hope that it helps

Helps you get through
Because I know
You can make it
Just like I did too
Keep moving forward
And do your best
This is only a chapter
Have faith it will end

TRAUMA

Your brain can't actually
Function properly
It's constantly
Sending an alarm
To your body
That there is a threat
That somehow you are in danger
Even when you're not
It sends stress hormones
Through all of your veins
Which over-ride
The happy feel-good ones
Making you feel crazy
And insane

It sends the wrong signals
To your nervous system too
Causing so much chaos
Oh, what should you do
Your body is responding
Trying to keep you safe
Feeling so much fear
Instead of happiness

Your body stores all
Your old emotions

And trauma from the past
See, every time you get triggered
Your body is telling the story
From your past
All the sensations and feelings
That you feel inside
Are the stuff you ran from
Or the things you hide
When you don't process
Emotions or trauma
It stays in your body
There to just linger
Ready for the next time when
Something triggers
Them awake
Now until you start dealing
With them
In a healthy way
Through getting support
And some therapy
You will carry on going
Through the feelings
Again, and again
Until you break that cycle
And start healing
So, you see
Trauma isn't just about
Mental health

It's in your body
It's physical as well
It affects your mind, brain
And your body too
All of you
That's what trauma does
To you

Ending Of Chapters

At the end of a chapter
you feel it alright
things start to feel different
inside and out
You get this deep feeling
that things aren't right
like suddenly realising
this isn't your path
It feels so wrong
and it doesn't make sense
you feel so lost
and confused about life
Start asking yourself questions
what is this life all about
You start looking for the answers
And your solutions
From yourself inside
Because no one knows you better
Than you
Yes, that's right
You have all your answers
You know what's right
This is your journey
This is your life
So, when the chapter
Comes to an end

Know in your heart
Another will begin
You are the author
You get to write
A brand-new story
In your book
Of your life
Take control
Pick up a pen
And start to write
Write it how you want it
And don't settle for less
You are worthy
And you are enough
So, write a good damn story
Living a life that you love

To My Readers...

I really hope you have enjoyed my second collection of poems, and I hope my story has helped you through yours.

If you are going through a difficult chapter in your life, never give up, and know it will come to an end.

There is always hope.

Thank you for reading, and if you did enjoy this book, please would you be kind enough to leave a review where you purchased it. That would mean the world to me.

Love,

M. S. Aldrich

Acknowledgments

Thank you to my family for all your love and support, my love for you gave me the strength to carry on. Thank you to Jen and Katie for proof reading and all your help and support, I very much love and appreciate you.

Thank you to Amanda for formatting and the cover design @ www.letsgetbooked.com

ABOUT THE AUTHOR

M. S. Aldrich lives in Yorkshire with her husband, their kitty and two rescue dogs. She is a Mum and a Nanna and loves spending time with her family more than anything.

She started writing poems by sheer accident; after writing a letter to her late Mum to help with the grieving process, she realised that she had in fact written a poem. So, she has been writing poems ever since, as an expression of all her thoughts, feelings and emotions straight from her heart and out through her hands.

When she is not writing, she loves spending time outdoors; walking in the countryside, enjoying gardening, bike riding, swimming, listening to music and reading.

A highly sensitive person who feels all the feels.

You can find M.S. Aldrich on linktr.ee/msaldrich

Facebook - M.S.Aldrich

Instagram -@msaldrichpoet